When Winter Comes

by Nancy Van Laan

illustrated by Susan Gaber

An Anne Schwartz Book
Atheneum Books for Young Readers
New York London Toronto Sydney Singapore

Where oh where do the leaves all go
when winter comes and the cold winds blow?

The leaves go tumble
tumbling down.
Snow is their blanket.
Their bed is the ground.

Where oh where do the flowers go
when winter comes and the cold winds blow?

Their petals wilt,
but their seeds burrow down
to rest underneath
the leaves' golden crown.

Where oh where do caterpillars go
when winter comes and the cold winds blow?

Inside their cocoons,
so tightly wound,
waiting for spring
to bring green to the ground.

Where oh where do the songbirds go
when winter comes and the cold winds blow?

South, they fly,
warm-weather bound
to bask in the sun
on the soft, mossy ground.

Where oh where do the field mice go
when winter comes and the cold winds blow?

Field mice tunnel
under the ground
and rest in a nest
thick with thistledown.

Where oh where do the dappled deer go
when winter comes and the cold winds blow?

Dappled deer wander,
making no sound.
They rest, closely knit,
under trees, in a mound.

Where oh where do the fish all go
when winter comes and the cold winds blow?

Deep under they swim
when the pond's icebound.
In the dark, they
quietly circle around.

Where oh where does our little one go
when winter comes and the cold winds blow?

In a warm, warm bed
when winter comes round,
listening to the wind
with its gusting sound,
watching the snow
as it falls to the ground.

Snuggling deep.
Fast asleep.

For my first little grandbaby
—N.V.L.

*For Lauren, Marc, Sean, Sam, Danielle,
Nolan, Kate, Nina, and Ethan*
—S.G.

Atheneum Books for Young Readers
An imprint of Simon & Schuster Children's Publishing Division
1230 Avenue of the Americas
New York, New York 10020

Book design by Michael Nelson
The text of this book is set in Wilke Roman.
The illustrations are rendered in acrylic on Bristol board.

Printed in Mexico.
5 6 7 8 9 10

Library of Congress Cataloging-in-Publication Data
Van Laan, Nancy.
When winter comes / by Nancy Van Laan; illustrated by
Susan Gaber.—1st ed.
p.   cm.
"An Anne Schwartz Book."
Summary: Rhyming text asks what happens to different animals and
plants "when winter comes and the cold winds blow."
ISBN 0-689-81778-9
[1. Winter—Fiction. 2. Animals—Fiction. 3. Stories in rhyme.]
I. Gaber, Susan, ill. II. Title. PZ8.3.V47Wh   2000   [E]—dc21
97-32914